The Good-Hearted Youngest Brother

# The Good-Hearted Youngest Brother

An Hungarian Folktale
Translated by Emöke de Papp Severo
Pictures by Diane Goode

BRADBURY PRESS          SCARSDALE, N. Y.

Library of Congress Cataloging in Publication Data
The Good-hearted youngest brother.
Translation of A jószívú legényke.
SUMMARY: The youngest of three brothers is able to free three beautiful princesses from
their enchantment because of his kindness.
[1. Folklore — Hungary]   I. Severo, Emöke de Papp.
II. Goode, Diane.
PZ8.1.G6357      398.2'1'09439      [E]      80-28169
ISBN 0-87888-141-7

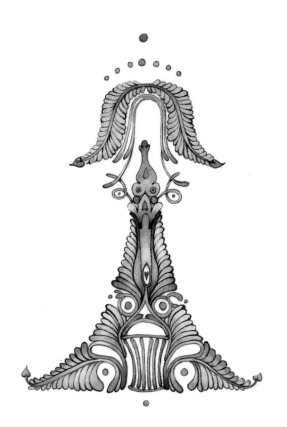

For my mother and father — *E. de P. S.*
For Peter Goode — *D.G.*

NCE THERE WAS, where there was not, seven times seven countries beyond where the bob-tailed piglet roots, a youngest brother with two older brothers. They were very good brothers.

When their father and their mother died, nothing remained to them except two guns.

"How are we going to divide two guns among three sons?" asked the older brothers.

"Let them be yours," said the youngest brother. "It's enough for me if you two just continue to be my good brothers."

And so it happened that the two older brothers took the two guns and with their younger brother set out to seek their fortune.

They wandered and meandered far, far — until they arrived
at a large forest, where thousands upon thousands of wild doves
were fluttering.

"I'll just shoot down a couple of wild doves," said the oldest
brother. "At least we'll have a tasty roast."

"Don't hurt them, dear brother," begged the youngest one.
"They've never done us any harm."

The oldest brother lowered his gun and they went on.

They wandered and meandered far, far — until they reached a green lake on which thousands upon thousands of loons were swimming and diving.

"I'll just shoot a pair of loons," said the middle brother. "We haven't had a tasty roast our entire trip."

"Please don't shoot the poor loons," begged the youngest brother. "They've never done us any harm."

The middle brother obeyed him, too. And they went on.

They wandered and meandered far, far — until they reached a large meadow. In the middle of the meadow was a bush and on the bush three beautiful, but very beautiful blossoms: a lily, a carnation, and a rose.

"What beautiful flowers," exclaimed the two older brothers. "Let's pluck them."

"Don't pluck them," begged the youngest brother. "They would just wither away."

But the two older brothers reached for the flowers anyway.

All of a sudden, a tiny rabbit jumped out from the bush. Silver was his fur, golden his ears, diamond his eyes. He lunged at the two older brothers with such force that they fell flat on their backs. When they got up again, they were afraid to pluck any flowers and they continued on their way.

They wandered and meandered and in a little while they reached a small house. Inside, they found not one living soul.

"How good it would be to find a bite of something tasty," said the oldest brother.

In a blinking of an eye the table was laid with grilled meats, cakes, and every which kind of good food and drink.

How they marvelled at this! But they were very hungry and didn't marvel long. Instead, they set to and had such a good feast that their ears stood in two directions.

Then the youngest said: "And now it would be good if we could thank someone for all these blessings."

Just then, into the little house jumped a little man. A hand's span height was the man, a hundred yards long his beard and he yelled:

"*Hey, hey!*"

The boys just stared at him. One was more frightened than the other and they said not one word.

The little man again started his yelling, but this time angrily: "*Hey, hey!*"

"Hey, hey, elegant little uncle," shouted the youngest brother. "We thank you for the good supper."

"Well, you're lucky that this child dared to open his mouth," said the handspan man, "because it would soon have been the end for all of you."

Thereupon, he immediately led the young men to an enormous, beautiful marble palace. The courtyard was full of hundreds upon hundreds of stone horses on which sat hundreds upon hundreds of stone soldiers. They went up the marble staircase and on the terrace were hundreds upon hundreds of stone men.

They entered a large, empty room. There were three golden chairs in the middle of the room. No one sat in them.

"Do you see those three chairs?" asked the handspan man. "They are the chairs of three forever bewitched, forever beautiful princesses, each of whom had a pearl and a crown. The three pearls are forever hidden inside three wild dove's eggs and the three crowns are forever at the bottom of the green lake. The three princesses will forever be the three beautiful flowers you saw on the bush in the middle of the meadow.

"Unless," the handspan man continued, "someone finds the pearls and the crowns and then guesses which of the three flowers is the eldest princess, which the middle, and which the youngest and then — in proper order, from the oldest to the youngest — places on each one a pearl and then a crown. *That* someone will be the one to undo the terrible bewitchment.

"But he who makes just one mistake at once turns into stone, as you can see all around you."

The handspan man paused. "So which one of you wants to break the spell?"

Each of the three brothers eagerly beat his breast. Each said that if he should live so long, he would surely break the terrible spell.

The eldest set out first, but no matter how he searched he could find neither the pearls nor the crowns and he turned to stone.

The middle brother's fate was exactly the same.

Finally, the youngest brother tried his luck. He wandered, he meandered, but no matter how he searched, how many trees he climbed, not even the broken shell of one wild dove's egg could he find.

Now he was doomed, too!

The youngest brother sat down on a tree stump and burst into bitter tears.

As he was weeping and wailing earnestly, a wild dove fluttered down beside him and said:

"Don't weep, don't wail, good-hearted young man. You took pity on us; we will take pity on you. Here are the three eggs for which you have been searching."

How happy the young man was! He thanked the wild dove for his goodness and went on to the green lake.

"But how am I going to raise the three crowns from the depths of the lake?" he groaned. "Even though I have the three pearls, I am still doomed."

The youngest brother sat down at the edge of the lake and burst into tears.

As he was weeping and wailing earnestly, a loon fluttered down beside him and said:

"Don't weep, don't wail, young man. Here are the three crowns from the bottom of the green lake. You see, it is not for nothing you have a good heart."

How happy the young man was! He thanked the loon for his goodness and went on to the large meadow where the three beautiful flowers bloomed.

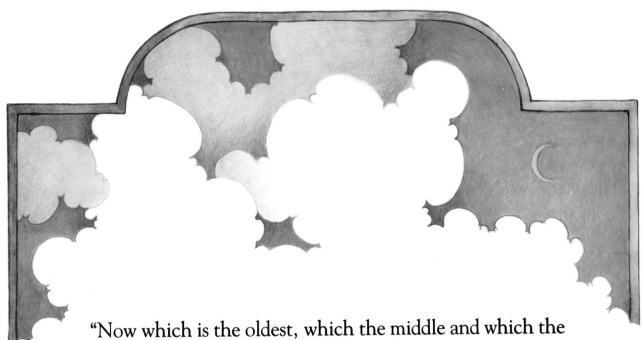

"Now which is the oldest, which the middle and which the youngest princess?" he groaned.

The youngest brother stood there for the entire day, just looking, looking at the flowers, not daring to touch any of them.

In great despair, he gave way to bitter tears. As he was weeping and wailing earnestly, the tiny, silver-furred, golden-earred, diamond-eyed rabbit jumped right before him and said:

"Don't weep, don't wail, young man. Listen to my words: the lily is the oldest, the carnation the middle, and the rose the youngest princess."

How happy the young man was! In prompt and proper order, he hung each pearl around the stem of each flower, placed each crown on each flower's head — and in a blinking of an eye the flowers turned into three forever beautiful, forever un-bewitched princesses.

And at that very same moment, the entire countryside came to life: the hundreds upon hundreds of stone horses, stone soldiers, stone men, and the two stone brothers all started breathing, chatting, laughing. Even the tiny rabbit turned into a proper, shapely young man — and the handspan man, too.

The good-hearted youngest brother married the youngest princess; the two older brothers married the two older princesses.

After that, they lived a very long time, and if they haven't died, they are living still.